# SLAMMED

HARGED

# SLAMMED

## HONDA CIVIC

Patrick Jones

MINNEAPOLIS

Text copyright © 2013 by Lerner Publishing Group, Inc.

Darby Creek
A division of Lerner Publishing Group, Inc.
241 First Avenue North
Minneapolis, MN 55401 U.S.A.

Website address: www.lernerbooks.com

The images in this book are used with the permisison of:
Cover and interior photograph © Transtock, Inc./Alamy.

Main body text set in Janson Text LT Std 12/17.
Typeface provided by Linotype AG.

Library of Congress Cataloging-in-Publication Data

Jones, Patrick, 1961–
    Slammed : Honda Civic / by Patrick Jones.
        pages    cm. — (Turbocharged)
    Summary: "After getting out of reform school, DeAndre lands back in the life that put him there: racing souped-up cars with stolen parts. But in trying to earn back his Detroit cred—and his girlfriend—he'll learn what it really means to win."—Provided by publisher.
        ISBN 978–1–4677–1245–3 (lib. bdg. : alk. paper)
        ISBN 978–1–4677–1670–3 (eBook)
        [1. Automobile racing—Fiction. 2. Honda automobile—Fiction. 3. Muscle cars—Fiction. 4. Conduct of life—Fiction. 5. Racially mixed people—Fiction.] I. Title.
    PZ7.J7242Sl 2013
    [Fic]—dc23                                     2013001967

Manufactured in the United States of America
1 – BP – 7/15/13

TO THE EPM

# CHAPTER ONE

*Tick. Tick. Tick.*

I stared at the clock in the classroom.
Next to the clock was a small window to the
outside world, and beyond that window, a tall
fence with barbed wire. "When you're doing
time, time moves too slow," I whispered to
Jordan. He stifled a laugh, and the teacher
and the correctional officer—CO for short,
a fat, middle-aged white guy with an attitude
problem—both glared at him. Laughing was
something normal, something you did on the
outs, not inside at Maxey.

I pretended to talk with Jordan about this silly worksheet on science. The only science most guys needed to know was chemistry for their street pharms, but Jordan and I were different. We'd met this morning when we moved into the STAR cottage. We got into it over a *Super Street* magazine but bonded on cars straight off. "What's the fastest you ever got your ride?" I asked.

Jordan wrote on the worksheet. *125.*

I nodded my head in approval. He nodded back, and his dreads danced. There were two kinds of guys: guys like Dad, who loved cars, and guys like me and Jordan, who loved to race. The cars were means, and my Civic was my power machine.

"DeAndre Taylor, Jordan White, focus!" The CO was onto us. "You're STARs, so act like it." The teacher, Mrs. T, looked peeved—her normal state.

"Yes, sir!" we replied automatically. Jordan and I had just started in the STAR program: Successful Transition Averts Recidivism. We were both headed home in a week, and for this last week, we'd do all this stuff to make sure we didn't reoffend. To me, the letters were right but in the wrong order: we were RATS. Most of Detroit, especially my side, the east side, was a rattrap. Dogs running wild, the police running scared, and people dying a little bit every day.

Once Ms. T started up again—I wouldn't call what she did teaching, but I didn't listen much—I poked Jordan's bare arm to get his attention. His black skin wasn't tagged with a green *Eastside Power Machines* tat like mine was.

"Why you in?" I asked.

"Stealing stuff for my ride, and to sell to my hookup."

"What's your ride?" I whispered. On the outs, sure enough he'd show me pix on his phone. Instead of saying anything, he drew a picture on my worksheet. Honda Civic.

I smiled with all my crooked teeth. "Mine, too, except it's slammed."

"How much it cost?" he wrote on the worksheet.

I drew dollar signs, but no numbers. "I did it." Lowering  the car myself was the only way I could afford it.

Jordan looked impressed. "You race too?" he whispered.

I nodded. I didn't just race, I was a racer. It wasn't something I did; it was who I was.

"I knew all the guys who race downriver, where I used to live," Jordan said. I'd heard that, but kind of like gangs kept to their own turf, the same was true with racers.

"DeAndre, Jordan, pay attention!" the teacher shouted in her gear-grinding voice.

I said nothing back, which was largely how I'd made it through seven months, three days, and ten hours at Maxey Boys' Reform School. On the outs, I was a show-off, but in here, I kept my mouth shut, ate their garbage rules, and swallowed their disrespect. I looked up at the clock and then stared at the Civic drawing.

Instead of *tick, tick, tick,* I heard *vroom, vroom, vroom.*

# CHAPTER TWO

## EIGHT MONTHS EARLIER.

*Thwack. Thwack. Thwack.*

*LT held his hands high at the ready to signal the start of the race, but then he waved them in frantic circles. Ali and I stuck our heads out of our cars—my slammed Honda Civic and his modified Acura Integra—to see four Detroit Police choppers blocking the moon and hovering over us, the other racers, and the crowd. The spotlights shot down on us like lasers.*

*The roar of the blades drowned out the bass beats booming from cars lining Industrial Drive. The old Ford factory along this street used to* make cars, but now we just raced in the streets in front of it.

"DeAndre!" Ali shouted and then pointed in front of and behind us. Cop cars descended on us like an invading army.

"The cops—go go go!" Everyone shouted at once, but nobody shouted louder than LT. It was like somebody turned on the lights in my mom's kitchen: we scattered like cockroaches.

The cars lining the roadside split, but Ali and me were at the starting line with LT. We jumped out of our cars and got LT into Ali's Acura. When I got back to my ride, I saw we were surrounded. Ali floored it, but too little, too late, and two cop cars blocked him. Two more moved closer to me.

We'd heard rumors that the cops planted a snitch, and this raid proved it. We'd moved the track several times tonight, so the only way the DPD could've known was if somebody said something. LT didn't let many folks into his inner circle, just Ali. I was close, but I still needed to earn back his total trust. I knew he'd blame me for this bust unless I did something.

I sat in my car, gunned the engine, and

watched it go down like a movie.

"Out of the car!" a voice growled through a speaker. With the sky red from cherry tops, it was like the devil had landed in Detroit. They'd blocked the street ahead and behind with cruisers while cops climbed out of vans to arrest spectators. "Out of the car!"

I opened the door and took one step out. When the cops got out of their car and were two feet away, I jumped back in my Honda, floored it, and took aim. My bumper snapped the doors off the two cop cars surrounding me, and then, like twigs on a tree, broke off the ones in the cars trapping Ali. The police scampered back into their now-two-door black-and-whites.

As I led the chase, I knew there was no getaway route here—just a road jammed with attacking cops and retreating street racers. To the east was the rubble of a factory, while west was a fenced-in empty parking lot. I spotted the driveway of the parking lot, spun a circle around the cop cars, and then smashed through the fence. All my icy bodywork was ruined, but I'd saved Ali and LT. I saw red lights behind me and yellow chopper lights above me, but in my mind all I saw was a green light that flashed: "Drive, DeAndre, drive!"

As I raced away, sparks flew from under the car. Being low to the ground made it handle like a dream and race like a rocket, but my slammed Honda wasn't built for this pitted parking lot. My head smashed hard into the top of the car while my nose filled with the vapors of burning tires, billowing exhaust fumes, and salty sweat. With four cars behind me and a helicopter above me, I was in the center of attention. As the speedometer clocked into triple digits, for a split second I stared at Nikki's photo on the dash: small brown eyes, wide, painted red lips, and straight teeth. She made my heart beat faster, but as I pushed the pedal to the floor, not even the thought of her made my heart beat this loud.

# CHAPTER THREE

"While you look good in that gold shirt, tomorrow you wear what you want," said Mr. Ryan, my transition social worker. I nodded. As always, I said as little as possible, getting by on grunts, nods, and fake smiles. "You earned that gold." The clothes we wore at Maxey were blue, except the week before you left.

"DeAndre, is it okay if we review your discharge plan again?" It was another stupid question from a middle-aged, balding white guy, answered by another nod from me. My entire stay at Maxey condensed into one last one-way conversation.

"Now, the condition of your release includes a year on probation. If you are arrested again in that year, or violate the other terms, then it's back inside. Not here, but a state prison, probably. It's up to the judge. Really, it's up to you. You understand what I'm saying?"

My neck hurt from nodding so much. My jaw ached from faking this smile one last time.

"And what are those terms, DeAndre?"

I stared at my county-issued Converse-rip-off blue kicks. "I can't drive."

"Or..."

"Or have any part in races," I added.

"Right. But don't worry, I've got something for you." He reached into the desk between us and searched for something, and I thought how there was a lot more than the desk separating us. I bet this guy didn't grow up on the east side of Detroit. I bet he'd gone to a good school with a killer auto shop. I bet he'd had all the stuff I never had. People always told you that you got as good a shot as anyone, but it seemed like the people saying that drove Beemers while folks like my mom had busted-up, rusted-out Buicks.

I didn't make eye contact, even as Mr. Ryan handed me the small envelope. "It's a bus pass."

I grunted something that sounded like "thank you." I took the pass from the envelope.

"The key to successful reentry," he droned on like a robot, "is avoiding the people, situations, and settings that led to your incarceration. But it is all about choices." He paused. "You understand?"

Another nod, head down so he wouldn't see the smirk that I couldn't hide. He said these words like it was possible: I was headed back to the hood with the same people, but somehow everything was supposed to be different. He was a social worker. I needed a miracle worker.

"You can use the pass to meet with your probation officer, Mr. Backus, once a month."

I didn't even bother to nod again. I was out in a day, so the rules they put on me—what I could say, eat, read, watch, and think—they didn't matter. Only LT's rules mattered now.

"Your credits will transfer when you go back to school. Going back to school is what?"

"Another condition," I answered. Truth was, it was my mom's condition too. The only way she said I could come home after this was to stay in school. Nobody in my family had ever graduated, so she wanted me to be the first. I'd messed up so much, I owed her something.

"Any questions, DeAndre?"

I laughed inside. I had a thousand questions, but none this guy could answer. I didn't think Mr. Ryan knew, for example, why Nikki stopped writing or wouldn't see me on my home visits. I knew he couldn't tell me how Ali, LT, and the rest of the guys would react when I saw them again. "Do you know what happened to my ride?" I asked.

"Why would you ask that, DeAndre? If you start racing again, then—"

"Look, it's my ride. I put a lot into it. It's mine, and nobody can take that away."

"Well, DeAndre, the county did. It's impounded, and if you want it back, then—"

"A lot of bills."

Mr. Ryan nodded this time.

I had a gold shirt but no green.

Mr. Ryan stood and started to walk away. "Make better choices, DeAndre," he said as I crumpled the bus pass in my hand.

# CHAPTER FOUR

Mom and I didn't talk much on the ride from
Maxey. I wanted to listen to music and look
out the window of her old Buick to distract
myself. I hated how Mom drove: too slow and
always braking at yellow lights.

The second we walked into our tiny
apartment, Mom started up. "I bought you a
bike," she said.

"Seriously, a bike."

Mom hung her coat neatly on a rusting
hook. I tossed mine on a chair. "Yes,
DeAndre, a bike. They took away your license,

so you won't be driving, and I don't have time to be running you around. This is another consequence of your actions. Maybe you'll learn something."

"Where's my phone? I gotta hit some people up."

"You're back in this house ten seconds, and already you're planning on leaving again?" she said, half-angry and half-sad. "That's going to change too. I don't want you hanging with those same guys. I've transferred you to a new school. And no more late nights."

I scoffed and sighed but wanted to spit. "Like you're one to talk."

She said nothing and walked into the kitchen. Mom worked two jobs, but she also partied. How come was she asking me to change when she kept doing the same things? She came out a few minutes later with my phone. She held it in front of her like a gift.

"After dinner." She tucked it into her pocket. We talked about nothing much as she heated up dinner—leftovers from the hospital cafeteria where she works.

"How about Nikki? Can I see her?" I lifted up a spoonful of fake mashed potatoes.

"I like Nikki," Mom said, thinking and chewing. "Her father's a dentist, right? I wonder if she's still in choir at church." I grunted and shrugged. "Don't you know?" Mom asked.

"Well, she must have went away or somethin' this summer, 'cause she never wrote back." I stared down at my food.

"Probably doing something positive for her community. You could learn from her."

Nod, spoon, chew, swallow. Home seemed a lot like Maxey.

"Anyway, they said your credits from East and Maxey will transfer to Carter Woodson Academy. I think it'll be good for you. It's a charter school that focuses on students like you," she said.

I looked up. "Like me *how*?"

She rushed some food into her mouth and chewed for a minute before answering. "You could study harder."

"I don't care about school. None of it's real to me. I'm going be a mechanic—that's the only course I care about. Not other garbage." I wanted to become a racer, but I never said that part aloud.

"The school has a program in auto mechanics, so that should make you happy."

Mom knew I liked cars but hadn't known I raced 'em until I got popped. They busted me on speeding, evading arrest, trespassing—a bunch of stuff, but no felonies. They tried to get me to say that I stole cars and parts, but I said nothing. Too bad that the one thing I'm good at—fixing up cars, wherever the parts come from—I can't tell her about to earn some respect.

"I'm going to the library after dinner," I announced.

Mom almost choked on her food. "That's a change for the better."

"When I was locked up, I read every *Super Street*, *Hot Rod*, and *Motor Trend* magazine at Maxey. Then I started on books. So, I can change. Don't worry about me, Mom."

"That's what moms do." She handed me the phone and started clearing the table. As

soon as she ran water to wash the dishes, I
headed toward my room. Everything was the
same. All my racing posters, pictures of Nikki,
and car models like I left them. I powered up
the phone. The first thing I did was call the
impound lot, but it was closed. Next I called
LT, then Nikki, but neither of them picked up.
Finally I texted Ali to meet me at the library
in thirty.

# CHAPTER FIVE

"Meet us tonight off Industrial and we'll go,"
I shouted at the Asian guy in the Acura next
to Ali and me. That guy's car wasn't as tricked
out as Ali's, but it looked like it could jam.

He flipped us off. "C'mon, race me here
and now."

"You wanna go?" Ali shouted over me, the
music, and common sense. I'd told him if I got
caught racing with him, I'd be violating my
parole and get bounced back. He didn't care.

"Don't do it, Ali!" I warned. But he wasn't
looking at me. Like the guy next to us, he just

looked straight up at the red light, waiting for green. "Come on, Ali, we don't do this. We don't race 'em daylight."

"You never did." That was true, but about nobody else did either. At least, not since the time Cory and LT raced a hundred miles an hour down a city street in the middle of the day. LT crashed while Cory killed a kid.

Ali gunned the engine, and the noise exploded inside my head. The second the light turned green, it was on. Ali got the lead at first, but he wasn't timing the shifts. It's not just about the ride—it's about the driver. "Hang on, DeAndre!"

He shifted into overdrive, but it wasn't enough. The Asian guy beat us to the next light on Ten Mile Road by less than two seconds. Ali cursed as the guy sped away.

"I had too much weight in the car," he said. I laughed, but he didn't. Ali had an answer for everything. "Don't you tell nobody about this, DeAndre. Keep your mouth shut."

I let it go. "Where we going?" I asked.

"LT's, but we gotta make a stop first."

"Alright."

"So, you don't wanna race no more?" Ali asked. "You scared straight or something?"

I laughed. "You know I don't like running them in the streets during the day," I reminded him. "I'll smoke anybody after midnight, but not on the streets like this."

"You afraid of getting caught?" Ali asked.

"Doing time wasn't so bad. I missed Nikki, and seeing your ugly face."

Ali didn't laugh. He wasn't ugly, but he did have a big scar on his forehead courtesy of a crash. But just because racing hurt you didn't you mean you stopped doing it. Like LT said once, why not live large in the short term rather than living small for the long term?

Ali turned the music down as we pulled up in front of a fancy mall near the church I used to attend. He gave me a hard look. "Since you got busted, nobody talks about racing in front of civilians. You got that?"

"Sure thing."

"One more thing. Remember you was gone nine months." He honked the horn twice.

"Eight months, why?"

Ali honked again and got out of the car. A second later I could see it clearly through the tinted windshield: Ali was standing with my Nikki hanging on his arm, like a catfish on the end of the line.

# CHAPTER SIX

"We straight?" Ali asked me as soon as Nikki left half an hour later. She hadn't breathed a word to me until she said good-bye when we dropped her at her big house off Cass Ave.

"It's cool, right, DeAndre?" Ali said before I could answer his first question.

"We good," I said. Not like I had a choice, but I was going take the full beating like a man. I even moved from the back to the front and sat next to him. "So how'd you two hook up?"

"Just happened. But there's one thing I know—I ain't gonna let happen to me what

29

happened to you." Ali laughed, while I growled inside like a hungry, angry lion. Nikki was barely inside her house before Ali started texting her. "Gots to keep her on the short leash, know what I'm saying?"

"Seems like you're the one she's got on the leash," I said and managed a smile.

Ali stopped the car, backed up, and put it in neutral. He revved the engine three times and then slammed it into gear, leaving a familiar cloud of exhaust and burnt rubber behind. I felt sick about Ali and Nikki, but I welcomed the familiar smell. I breathed in deep and relaxed a little.

Ali's phone lit up. LT's ring. He listened for a second, then started to talk loudly. "You should've seen it LT, on the way over, I smoked this lame Acura." Ali would rather climb a tree to a lie than stand on the ground and tell the truth. He couldn't snitch, because nobody believes a word he says. Well, most everybody. To LT, Ali's gold, 'cause he's a loyal follower and a fool.

While Ali told his story, I closed one

chapter of mine by deleting Nikki's number from my phone. Then I called the impound lot again. Nikki broke my heart, but the impound fee broke my spirit.

※ ※ ※

We pulled into LT's auto garage, which did legal work by day and turned into chop shop at night. After LT asked about my time at Maxey, I got to the point. "I need two thousand bills to get my ride out of impound."

"You left it there when you were inside?" LT asked. Ali laughed. Two of LT's groupies, Cal and Michael, stopped working on LT's Mazda RX7 to laugh. "I'll loan at twenty percent interest," LT offered.

I shook my head. "No, I wanna earn it."

"How you gonna do that without a car?" LT asked.

"Win it, bets. I met this guy inside who told me about some hot action downriver."

"You gonna race your bike?" Ali asked. Everybody laughed but me.

"Maybe I could borrow a car," I said really low, almost a whisper.

"Not my ride," Ali said.

LT hesitated. "I've heard about downriver, but it's a real tough crowd," he said. "You sure you want to do this?"

I nodded.

"You can use my RX," LT said, to surprised stares. "But you'd better win— without wrecking it."

"LT, why you lettin' DeAndre represent us? That should be me," Ali said.

I laughed at Ali. "I ain't shifted a gear in eight months, and I'm still better than you."

Ali stepped toward me, but LT got between us. "You think you're better than DeAndre? Prove it. Saturday night. We'll meet out by the closed Kmart and find a place that's not hot."

I just nodded. Ali turned his back to me and popped the hood of his Acura. Just the smell of the engine vapors made my head dizzy with happiness. "Thanks, LT."

He nodded and then stared at his RX7 the way I looked at Nikki.

"You miss racing, LT?" I asked.

"Every day," LT said softly. He ran the fingers of his left hand gently over the rims on the custom chrome wheels of the RX and then did the same to the big rims on his wheelchair.

# CHAPTER SEVEN

"Sweet chrome," some Asian guy said to me.

"It's his ride." I pointed at LT and then went back to work getting his wheelchair out of the backseat. LT moved easily from the car to the chair, chatting with the Asian guy the whole time.

While LT sat like a proud papa in front of his RX7, I joined in with Michael, Cal, and others walking the circuit. I had my flashlight in hand as I inspected engines of cars I'd never seen before or that had been modified. I wished my old auto mechanics teacher could see the magic we worked on these cars, but I didn't think he'd appreciate it since most of these modifications were illegal.

The parking lot of the closed Kmart was an oasis of racers. Not everybody raced. Some guys just liked to show off their cars, and other guys liked to show off their girls. I'd never asked Nikki to come watch me race or to show off like these other guys did with their girlfriends. Ali told me he'd bust her up if she even thought about showing skin like that for anyone other than him.

My senses were working overtime as I walked around. My ears filled with reverbing bass, revving engines, and challenges issued. My nose tickled with burning rubber from the drifters, the scent of oil and gasoline, and the smell of weed. My mouth tasted of metal.

"Hey, DeAndre!" I heard somebody shout. I turned. Jordan, from Maxey, stood next to a white Honda. It wasn't slammed or tricked out, but it still looked like a fine ride.

"What you doing up here?" I asked.

"I thought I'd check you guys out. With all

that trash-talking you did at Maxey, I figured you'd want to try your luck downriver. So I'm scouting you, I guess."

"Luck won't have nothing do it with—it's all skill." I motioned shifting gears. Jordan laughed, and we looked under the hood of his car. I held my flashlight in my mouth so I could touch everything with both hands. Under a hood, I felt like a brain surgeon rather than some D student.

"You here with your friend? Ali, right?" Jordan asked.

I laughed. "Racing him tonight. But Ali's easy to find. Just look for LT's wheelchair, and Ali is one step behind. If LT stopped too quick, he'd break Ali's nose, it's shoved so far up—"

"Wait, wait, isn't this guy your friend?" Jordan asked, laughing. "Why you hang with him?"

I smiled. "He's more of a rival." I made no mention of Nikki. "Just old habits, I guess, plus I like LT."

"DeAndre!" LT yelled and waved me over. I left Jordan and ran back.

"I got the spot. We're lead." I nodded and then helped him back into his RX. "I'm gonna spread it." LT started to text, and I knew all over East Detroit, texts were bouncing around letting people know where we'd be racing.

"Thanks for letting me use your wheels," I said.

"Hey, at least I know you follow my rules." He'd raced for years, and the one time he didn't follow his code—raced on a busy street—he got hurt. No busy streets with civilians who would get in the way or call the police, and no races until after midnight.

From the sky, I bet we looked like the world's longest electric eel as we snaked slowly down city streets. We finally reached a long section of road not far from another closed factory—they lined Detroit like concrete dinosaurs. The racers headed to the south end, while spectators backed in and waited. Somebody marked off the quarter mile, and the racers started to line up.

As we eased our way up the line for our turn, Ali came and helped LT out of the RX.

LT wheeled himself down the middle of the road. He was going to spot us.

As I waited for Ali to get his car into place, I revved the engine. LT had built this RX from scratch after he crashed his old one in that race against Cory. We'd all helped with the physical work, but somehow when Ali talked about it, it was like the rest of us didn't exist. I guess I always figured that LT would know who did the work and who just took the credit. I had faith in LT, and I hoped he had faith in me. But at the starting line, all I needed was faith in his machine.

Finally, Ali pulled up at the starting line opposite me. As I stared over at Ali, I didn't see a friend; I saw the reason Nikki wouldn't even text me anymore. I'd lost my car and my love, but I would not lose this race. I needed to win. I hated to lose and feel like a loser.

Just like I'd waited out those last few seconds at Maxey, I bit my bottom lip as I waited for LT to say those three magic words: *ready, set, go!*

# CHAPTER EIGHT

I revved the engine and waited. My hands white-knuckled the wheel while my feet danced on the floor: left on the brake, right on the accelerator. Before me was open road offering a chance at glory and respect.

LT sat between both cars, his chair clouded in a mist of exhaust. In the rearview I saw the endless string of phones taking photos or shooting video. LT raised his right hand, paused, and dropped it to his side as Ali and I floored it. LT was the gun, his hands the trigger, and we were speeding bullets.

My engine roared, my tires screeched, and my heart pounded as I pushed on the clutch, slammed the car into first, and shattered the darkness in front of me. The shift into second hurled me back into my seat like I'd been pushed by one of my mom's drunk exes. Electricity ran through my veins, and I was part of the machine. I shifted into third. Another push, hoping it got me out in front. I didn't look to my side; there was no time. It wasn't about the other racer or the other car. Street racing was about you, your machine, and your desire to win.

I kicked into fourth, and under the hood, every wire, hose, and part strained under the pressure. LT's car hadn't been raced in a while, and when it had been, he'd only let Ali touch it. I wasn't just touching it; I was owning it.

My ankle ached as I let out the clutch and pressed the gas one more time, almost forcing it through the floor. Final gear and final seconds. My lungs sucked in fumes from LT's nitrous oxide-fueled RX like it was life-giving air. And as I crossed the finish line, I heard the sound of Ali's Acura a microsecond behind me.

I took my foot off the gas, let my machine coast, and opened the window. For all the heat from the tires, the engine, and the rush, this was the best: the cool of the evening after victory.

# CHAPTER NINE

"DeAndre, over here!" a voice called out to me from across the cafeteria on my first day at the Carter Woodson Academy. I pivoted like a point guard. It was Jordan.

I smiled and walked over. As I looked over some of the hard faces, tatted-up arms, and angry stares I passed, I could tell it'd be best if I stayed low like my ride. I yawned before we fist-bumped. I had to get up an hour earlier to get to school by bus.

"What you doing here?" he asked.

"Mom said this was the kind of school I

needed to change my ways."

Jordan laughed. "Me too, bro, 'cept . . ."

"Nothing has changed." I pointed at our uniforms and laughed. They were almost the same color as the ones we wore in Maxey. I didn't mind it, actually. Looking like everybody else would help me keep my head down, out of trouble, and focused on graduating. "But school's gotta be better than at Maxey."

He laughed. "I was surprised to see you still racing."

"One-time thing," I lied. Trust on the outs was different than when you're inside. "I noticed you didn't race. You downriver dudes scared of some real action?"

"Fact is, DeAndre, I was just telling stories. I tune, but I don't race." I shot him a puzzled look. "I love my ride, but I'm scared of crashing, of dying."

I lowered my voice. "Me, I'm scared of not living."

"Not living?"

"Listen, my dad played his whole life

safe. While almost everybody else on the block went to prison or worse, he stayed out, got a good job at the Apex Stamping Plant. His brother wanted him to quit the job and go half in on a garage, which ain't funny because my uncle wasn't half the mechanic Dad was, or I am. But Dad said no, I want to play it safe. That garage could have been mine one day, but Dad didn't want any risk. And then, like two weeks later, he's dead. Crushed by a stamping machine he was repairing."

I felt like crying, but I fought it.

"From the insurance, I bought my Honda. Then I fell in with my crew."

Jordan frowned. "I love my CRX too much to risk it. It's all I got."

"I hear people say that racing is risky, but that's only if you don't know what you're doing," I said, talking too much. "Life is all a risk anyway."

He shrugged. "True."

In the awkward quiet, I surveyed the landscape. "Say it ain't so, Jordan." He looked puzzled, while I shook my head like I'd been punched. "There are no girls here."

"Don't matter to me none. I got plenty back home, like you do. How's Nikki?"

More silence, and my broken heart skipped a beat. I decided to tell him the story, but tried not to say her name. When I said it, I heard her voice.

"But you're still friends with that guy? Man, you're one tough mo—"

"Racing is all I got. So I got nothing to lose."

"Except your life, or somebody else's." He smiled when he said it.

"Just mine. People who put civilians at risk are no better than bangers shooting into houses."

"We better get to class. You taking the auto mechanics course?" he asked. I nodded.

"Taking it, even though my dad taught me. He was more like a magician than a mechanic."

"My pops was a magician too," Jordan said. "'Cept his only trick was disappearing."

※ ※ ※

"I have only three rules," the auto shop teacher, Mr. Roberts, announced at the start of class. I looked over at Jordan, and we both laughed. Three rules was only about two hundred ninety-seven less than we'd had at Maxey. "Show up on time, work hard all hour, and have fun."

Jordan raised his hand. "But working hard ain't having fun." Some folks laughed.

Mr. Roberts put his hands on his hips, which was a chore since he had a lot of extra weight to pass by. "I think you'll find it is quite possible to do both. Fourth rule, don't use words like *ain't*."

"So now this is English class too? Do I get double credit?" More laughs.

"If you want to succeed in this world, gentlemen, you need to learn how to speak and act correctly in society. Talk however you wish with each other, but in here, use proper English. Now, gentlemen, if we're done talking, let's get to work. Coveralls in

46

that closet and cars are in the garage behind us. This class is all hands-on. Any more questions?"

I grabbed a pair of coveralls, slipped 'em on, and waited for Jordan. His didn't quite fit, which made me laugh, but that all stopped when we stepped into the garage behind us. There were twenty cars, all makes and models, hoods open and ready for work, but my eyes caught something else: around the garage, under lock and key, hundreds of parts on shelves. Jordan must've seen the same thing, 'cause he smiled and licked his lips like a hungry man seeing his dinner arrive.

# CHAPTER TEN

"Let's go again." Ali had been in my face the entire week for a rematch. Cal thought I should give him one; Michael said I had nothing to prove.

"Ain't gonna happen," I said.

"Man, you wouldn't even be racing if it wasn't for me," Ali said.

"I don't owe you anything," I said and wiped the grease off my hands. I was under the hood of LT's RX, getting ready to change out the fuel injector for the one he just bought.

Ali turned to Nikki, who was on his arm

again. "Did DeAndre tell you all I taught him when he started to hang here?" Nikki kind of shrugged. I'd told her my version of the story—that LT and his crew helped continue my education under the hood after my dad died. I was sure Ali had his own version. "Answer me!" he yelled.

Nikki flinched, and she started to walk away. He grabbed her by the wrist, hard. Pain shot across her face.

"Where are you going?" Ali shouted.

"Let her go," I said. I stared at her skinny arms covered with welts and bruises.

"Stay out of this, DeAndre. She's not yours now, she's mine."

"She doesn't belong to you." I knocked Ali's hand off Nikki's wrist, which allowed her to run out of the garage. I started to follow, but Ali grabbed my shoulder.

"You wanna go?" He bumped his chest against mine, even though he was about two inches shorter than me. As he jammed his finger into my shoulder, I knocked his hand away.

"Ali, DeAndre, enough!" LT shouted as he

wheeled up closer. Even though LT was seated, it seemed like he towered over Ali.

"Whatever you say," Ali said in the tone of a spoiled child.

"I'm out." I wiped my hands and walked out the door. Nikki stood by the street.

"You okay?" I asked her, keeping my distance. I never asked her why we ended. I figured if she wanted me to know, she'd say something. I learned when my dad died, you can fight 'em all you want, but if you don't accept the losses, you just lose yourself.

"I'm fine. I should go," Nikki said quietly.

"I'd give you ride, but my Civic's impounded until I get some cash. Lot of cash."

She stared at the street; I took a step closer. "Sorry, about that," she said. "About everything."

"Well, don't be saying the same thing to Ali. He should treat you better."

She shrugged, and her voice turned defensive. "You don't know what he's really like. He's so sweet to me," she said, softening. "He loves me." I could tell she believed what she was saying. But when I saw her start wiping tears, I headed back inside.

"Ali, I'll race you again, but only with some serious stakes."

"Problem with that, DeAndre, is you got nothing to lose. Nor do I," Ali said, all casual.

I looked at LT, Cal, Michael, and again at LT. Once my dad died, these people became my family and racing became my life. But where had that got me? Maxey and a broken heart. "Here's the stakes. We race again, and if you win, you get what I know you want."

"What's that?"

"I'm gone from here," I said. "But if I win, then you give up something."

"DeAndre, I'm not putting my ride on the table."

"No. You lose, you break it off with Nikki."

He laughed. "You think she'll come crawling back to you, you're wrong."

"Doesn't matter," I said. "I just know she deserves better." I looked him dead in the eyes. "Deal?"

Ali returned my stare, nodded, and shook my hand.

# CHAPTER ELEVEN

"I want to see it. Wish I could be there," Jordan said over the phone. His mom had him almost on house arrest. I walked around the closed Kmart lot, too nervous to sit in LT's RX7 and too distracted to focus on any other car.

"Don't risk it," I cautioned him. "LT's got a camera in the car. I'll upload the race."

"Too bad she took the other vids down."

"He probably made her." Before I went to Maxey, Nikki had posted lots of videos of me racing, but when I got out, they were all down, replaced by videos of Ali.

"That chick is whack."

I laughed. "I wouldn't know, I'm not an expert on females like you are."

Jordan laughed, but the sound of it got covered up in the explosion of sound from the lot. Engines revved, and seconds later I saw I had a text from LT. He'd found a place. It was time.

"Nikki's got about everything," I explained. "I guess she hangs with us 'cause we got nothing. She needs the excitement. Besides, her parents hated me, which probably helped me."

"You think they hate Ali?"

I paused and glanced at the text. "I don't know, but I'm sure starting to."

※ ※ ※

When I got back to the lot, cars were pulling out. LT said he'd ride with Ali at the front of the pack, so I waited and waited to be the last car out. We drove toward the river, and as we did, the surroundings started to look familiar. We were outside the Apex Stamping Plant, where my dad had worked. Where my dad died. Why did LT choose this place for this race?

LT texted to say we'd race around 1:00 A.M. He probably wanted some other people to go first just in case the cops were onto this or some civilians noticed. LT knew all the angles.

I stayed with people on the sides, shooting vids, snapping pix, and placing small side bets. I had some cash from Dad's social security checks, but Mom took most of it. She didn't want me to have enough to get my car out of impound. I should've put racing Ali off until I had my ride, but sometimes life didn't give you a choice. Life said go, and you put your foot to the floor.

Ali showed me he'd won a few more dollars. "You ready?"

"Where's Nikki?" I asked. He scowled like some banger posing for a mug shot.

"I told her to stay home."

I pretended I had a watch on my wrist. "Your time bossing her around is over."

"I'm gonna smoke you like a blunt, DeAndre."

From behind me, I heard LT. "So, DeAndre, is it the car or the driver that wins a race?"

"It's both. But I know this, LT, if I had my ride, we wouldn't be talking, because I would've beat Ali so bad last time, he'd still be home crying to his mama about it. It's the car and the driver."

"How much you got?" Ali pointed at my cash.

I shrugged. "Maybe a hundred."

"Why don't we do a side bet on our race. I say it's only the driver that matters."

"How you gonna prove that, Ali?" I asked.

Ali looked at LT, who nodded. Then Ali flipped me a set of keys. "We switch cars."

# CHAPTER TWELVE

"Ready. Set. Go!" LT shouted and signaled the race to start.

I slammed the gas, pressed the clutch, and hard-shifted Ali's Acura just like any other ride. He was off to a better start due to the new fuel injector in LT's RX, but I knew I'd catch him.

Until I saw the light. Oil pressure indicator, as bright as the taillights of Ali's car at the finish line.

I lost the bet because it was the wrong bet.

It wasn't about the kind of car or how

good of a driver somebody was. In every race, maybe every lap of life, it was the person behind the wheel. And when you competed against someone who would lie, cheat, steal, or even sabotage, you always lost.

I thought about crashing Ali's car, but I wouldn't go down to his level. I stopped the crippled car, took out the key, and then climbed out. I stood with the keys in one hand and the wad of bills in the other and waited under the Michigan moon for Ali to take everything from me.

Ali might have said something when he took the keys and the cash, but I couldn't hear him. I had my headphones on, and I never looked back as I walked away from the lights and action of that life.

# CHAPTER THIRTEEN

"Nobody?" Jordan asked when he geared his Honda down as we exited I-75.

"Nobody," I said, more to the floor mat than to Jordan. I'd told him how after the race, I hadn't heard from anybody in the racing crew, not even LT. I didn't hear from Nikki either. I couldn't figure exactly why she stayed with Ali, the way he treated her. But I knew how hard it is to give up something you love, even when it's the right thing to do. It was why I'd kept racing.

"So, you're sure you're okay with this?"

Jordan asked.

"I know you don't want to be back inside," I answered. "This doesn't violate my parole."

The downriver neighborhood looked a little better than around the east side, where I lived. There were fewer empty homes, less garbage on the street, and even businesses open, including Hautman Import Automotive. Jordan parked a block away. "Go to the back door."

I nodded and then took the cash from his hand. I didn't ask how he got it, but I didn't think he had a paper route or worked at McDonald's.

I knocked on the back door, and a tall white guy let me in. I handed him Jordan's order, and it took him a few minutes to gather it up. It was all small stuff: air filter, plugs. Nothing fancy. As the guy worked, I couldn't help but notice the car he had up: a black Civic. It looked a lot like mine, but I knew mine was still at the impound. I checked online every day to be sure.

"Nice ride. You slamming it for

somebody?" I asked. He grunted a yes.

"You using coilovers and putting it on steelies?" I took a step closer to inspect the work.

"He wants coilovers and wants rims. Gonna look like—"

"Garbage."

He half-laughed. "I just do what they tell me." He handed me a bag, and I handed him cash. I looked around this garage but thought about LT's garage and how I used to be just like that too.

"I got an idea," I said when I got back in the car. I put the bag on my lap.

"What's that?" Jordan asked.

"You should let me slam this Civic. It would be off the chain."

"No, I'd be on the hook, is what I'd be, with everybody in Detroit giving me a look. You tell me you used to ride around town in your Honda. Man, that's crazy. That's asking for trouble."

I laughed, but Jordan just stared at me. "What's so funny?"

"Riding around Detroit is asking for trouble, period."

Jordan nodded and eased the Civic into traffic. His work was mostly under the hood and some detail, but not enough to make it stand out. Even as he drove, he kept it cool. We leaned back in our seats as the bass pounded.

"Where you keep it?" I asked Jordan as we pulled off the expressway. "Even if I somehow get my ride back, I don't know where I'd work on it and store it."

"Here," he answered as he turned down a street in a nice neighborhood. Not quite like where Nikki lived, but nicer than where I lived. "It's my grandma's house—she doesn't mind."

"Really?"

Jordan opened the door and started out of the car. "She doesn't have one left."

"Have one of what left?" I asked out the window after him.

"A mind," he said and then opened the garage door. Inside was a temple of tools.

When he got back in the car, I asked,
"How'd you afford to buy all those tools?"
He laughed hard and shook his head.
"Who said I bought any of it?"

# CHAPTER FOURTEEN

I skipped school and went to see LT, since
I knew that Ali wouldn't be there. Like my
mom, Ali's mom was hard-nosed about him
going to class, but LT was older and done with
all that.

"LT, it's DeAndre." LT looked up from
his chair. He was changing the headlights
on his RX when I walked into the garage. I
knew he packed a heater, so I didn't want to
surprise him.

"DeAndre, what are you doing around
here?"

"I want to ask you something."

He set the headlight in his lap and wheeled his chair to face me. "I got nothing to say. You made a bet, you lost, and now you honor that bet. You best get movin'."

"Honor? Why should I honor a bet for a race that wasn't fair?"

"Cry to your mama, not to me."

"After all I've done for you, all the cars I've tuned, and all the races I've won for the EPM . . . and you treat me like this. I just want to know: did you know?"

"Know what?" His tone was odd because I'd never spoken to him like this before.

"You know what I mean," I replied. "Did you know that Ali was going to cheat me?"

"He won, you lost. End of story."

I grabbed his chair so he couldn't move. I put one foot on the chair, where LT's right leg would be, if he had one. "It wasn't fair!"

"Fair! Don't talk to me about fair, not when I'm sitting here like this." His eyes bulged.

"That's not what I meant. You of all people should know what happens when you let people do stuff you know is wrong," I said, almost in tears. "So why you gonna let something this wrong stand? How can you do nothing?"

"There's nothing I can do, unless you know how to build a time machine," LT said.

I grunted. "No, I don't know how to build that."

"Then maybe you should build something else."

"What's that?"

LT rocked in his chair and then pivoted the chair in a complete circle. He stared at his RX, the parts in the bins, and the tools on the table.

"LT, what are you saying?"

"That you should build a life better than this."

It was always hot in LT's garage, no matter what the weather, yet I felt a shiver. LT looked down where his right leg used to be and then looked at me the same way.

Then it was clear. "Wait. You? You *helped* him cheat me?"

He nodded and then fidgeted with the headlight like a baby with a rattle.

"Why would you help Ali sabotage the race?"

He reached into his front pocket and pulled out his wallet. He pulled something out of the wallet and held out a picture—one I'd never seen before. Of him and my dad.

"I owe your dad this. We went way back, but he never wanted you mixed up in the races. Then I watched out for you once he died, took you into my world. Wanted to give you a shot to get some cash and your ride back, racing the RX7. 'Specially since you took the heat for us. But then I realized that's just gonna keep you racing." He was a quiet for a minute. "I've got nothing else, but DeAndre, you don't need this. I knew you wouldn't leave, so I pushed you out."

"Pushed me out?"

"The race against Ali, the stakes, tricking you into switching, and messing with his car," LT said slowly. "Ali thought I was just playing favorites, teaming up with him. Truth is, I didn't want you to end up like me, or worse. I want you to have a chance at a better life than this. There's more to life than cars, girls, and racing. Now go find it!"

# CHAPTER FIFTEEN

"Let me see your arm."

"DeAndre, leave me alone!" Nikki hissed
at me. As she'd refused to answer texts, return
calls, or respond to messages, I'd decided I
had only one choice: confront her in person.
Knowing her dad would probably call the cops
if he saw me again, and her friends at school
probably felt the same, I did something I hadn't
done for almost a year. I went to church. She
was surprised to see me show up at the choir
practice, but she had to talk to me if she didn't
want to make a scene. We went outside.

"Nikki, you deserve better than Ali," I said. "You deserved better than me."

"Don't say that about yourself," Nikki said. She looked so pretty. How could someone so tiny have such a big voice?

"He's not going to change," I said.

"No, he's just—" she started and then stopped. She tugged at the long sleeve of the choir robe.

"Don't make excuses for him."

"DeAndre, this is none of your business. You don't own me. You just—for so long, you weren't there." She looked away. "It's nice to know Ali thinks about me so much. That he cares so much."

I knew it was time to tell her the stakes of the race, that Ali was willing to put their relationship on the line, even if the contest was rigged. I never took my eyes off her as I was explaining everything. When you race, even though it's only a matter of seconds, it's also like in slow motion. The speed of the car mixed with the rush of adrenaline seemed to slow down time and make every second more vivid, more memorable. I had that same sensation as I watched Nikki process what I told her. She seemed out of breath when I finished.

"I don't know what else to say," were my final words.

Before she could say anything else, I heard her phone vibrate.

"It's him, isn't it?" I asked.

She wiped her eyes, and the sleeve of her choir robe slipped down. I saw the colorful marks on her arm. I reached out and snatched the phone from her hand. I let it ring and go to voicemail. "Give it back."

"Take it back," I challenged her. "You want something, fight for it."

She stood in the evening sun while I scrolled through the phone. There were dozens of texts and missed calls from Ali in just the last twenty-four hours. "Nikki, why? Why do you stay with him?"

She said nothing. I knew from my time at Maxey this simple rule: if somebody asked you why you did or didn't do something, not answering didn't mean you didn't know.

Usually it meant you did, and the answer was just too shameful or painful to say out loud.

I handed her back the phone and then kissed both her cheeks, damp with tears.

✳ ✳ ✳

As I rode home on the bus, I pulled out my phone and the paper with the number I needed. I punched in the digits.

"You've reached the voicemail of Tom Backus, Detroit Juvenile Probation and Parole. I'm sorry I'm not available to take your call, so please leave a message."

"Mr. Backus, it's DeAndre Taylor," I said and then started fake-coughing. "I'm sick, so I can't make our meeting tomorrow. I should be better by next Monday."

A split second later, I called Jordan and got right to it. "So, you know when we left Maxey we had to say we'd change? I'm not sure either of us did."

"Look, DeAndre, all those tools I boosted before Maxey."

"In your toolbox, you think you got a pair of bolt cutters?"

"Why you asking?"

The bus pulled up to my stop, slowly. "How about one more boost and one more race?" I stood next to the driver. His cheap watch boomed in the mostly empty bus. *Tick. Tick. Tick.*

※ ※ ※

The next day, Jordan and I stayed late after school in the auto shop until Mr. Roberts told us he needed to lock up. We got all super-polite and headed toward the front door, but once we lost sight of anyone, we veered to the left and holed up in the bathroom, our feet on the toilets just in case the security guard came in.

We waited in total silence for a while and then slowly left the stalls and opened the door to the hallway. It was dark, empty, inviting. We made our way slowly and silently back to Mr. Roberts's room. The day before,

I'd lifted his keys first hour. Then we skipped second to get a copy made and then got 'em back in his desk before lunch. He probably never missed them.

The key worked perfectly. We walked quietly into the garage. I lifted the flashlight from my pocket and pointed it at the spot I'd memorized. Then I flashed the light in front of my face so Jordan could see my crooked-tooth smile, which made him laugh. "Shh!" I said.

The rest went so fast, I didn't even have time to think about getting busted. Jordan didn't say anything as he took off his jacket. I flashed the light at his chest, or more importantly, what he had strapped to his chest: bolt cutters. We got a ladder. He climbed it, while I held the ladder with one hand and the cutters with the other. The flashlight was in my mouth. Jordan tapped his foot on the steel ladder. The sound echoed in the darkness as I handed him the cutters. It was followed by another echo when he snapped the lock on the first try. He handed me back the bolt cutters.

I set them on the ground and then focused the flashlight on the shelf that was about to be missing one expensive part: a turbocharging kit. Once Jordan had it in hand, I put the flashlight back in my mouth and took the kit with both hands.

# CHAPTER SIXTEEN

"Good thing Grandma's checked out, or she'd have a fit that I skipped school last week," Jordan said.

I faked coughing again. "Well, tell her that you had to help a sick friend."

We laughed together as we sat in Jordan's car. It took almost the entire week, but his Civic was slammed and turbocharged. I waited to lay the smackdown on Ali.

We talked about girls, rides, sports, music—anything other than what we cared about: getting the text. After twenty more minutes, Jordan's phone buzzed. The meet-up tonight was outside Big Lots on Ecorse.

※ ※ ※

We arrived just before midnight. After Jordan parked, I walked toward the end of the lot where the races were being set up. Not everybody raced, so other people were checking out cars, or the girls by the cars. It was warm for a spring night, and most of the girls weren't wearing much. I found Ali's Acura, but he wasn't near it, nor was Nikki or LT. Cal and Michael stood like guards.

"What are you doing here?" Michael asked.

"Where's Ali?" I said.

"What do you care?" Cal jumped in.

"Challenge."

"With what? You get your ride out of impound?" he asked. I spit on the sidewalk.

"If he's too scared, I'll just let everybody know, especially Nikki. She doesn't like that."

Michael and Cal looked at each other, like

each hoped the other would decide. Finally Cal flipped his phone and texted. The answer took all of ten seconds. "Not interested."

"Who'd you text, Ali or LT?" Cal looked at the ground. "Now, call Ali."

This time Michael did the work; this time the answer was different. "Wait here."

I turned my back and sent two quick texts while I waited. Ali showed up without LT in front of him, but with Nikki right beside him. He palmed her backside like a basketball. She looked uncomfortable.

"I beat you, DeAndre, so beat it," Ali said with a smirk.

"Me and you, one more time." I stared right through him as I spoke. "Your ride vs. mine. Winner takes both cars, loser goes home on a bike. Bet?"

Ali nodded but wouldn't shake my hand. He looked lost without LT telling him what to do.

# CHAPTER SEVENTEEN

"You spotting it?" I asked LT. He shook his head. "One last time, I swear."

"That's what every addict says," he whispered hard. "I told you that—"

"No, LT, I'm really not—" but I didn't get any further before he rolled himself away. I tried to text Nikki, but she didn't answer and was lost in the crowd. I texted Jordan and asked him to look for her, but he was busy doing some last-minute tuning to his—our—slammed Civic.

Desperate, I ran through the maze of cars.

It was like I was inside one of those old-school pinball machines they used to have at the mall arcade. Lights flashed, music played, and even though the land was still, it felt like it was in motion under the weight of all this speed.

"Nikki! Nikki!" I shouted over the din, but there was nothing but loudness. I looked out over the controlled chaos and wondered how many other guys dreamed the same car-racing dream I did. I realized that if I ever did race, I'd only want to do drag racing. In drag racing, there was no past, just what was in front of you, and you got there as quickly as you could. In every other kind of racing, you just went around in circles and ended up where you started.

I wished that Ali didn't have tinted windows. I wanted to see the look on his face when I pulled up next to him in Jordan's Civic. Ali's car needed wings, because he didn't have a prayer. In front of us, a Mitsubishi Eclipse and a Subaru Impreza readied for battle. I'd blown away that Eclipse before.

I pulled up in the Honda Civic. Ali placed his Acura Integra. I was too afraid to blink.

# CHAPTER EIGHTEEN

*Tick. Tick. Tick.* The clock counted down.

*Vroom.* My engine was ready.

Cal, the starter in front of us, asked, "Ready? Set? Go!"

Blue flames shot from my exhaust and I was off. I heard nothing but my heart beating and my engine roaring; it was like I was half-deaf. With my eyes wide open, the street lay before me and I ate up one section of road at a time.

Four seconds gone, and fourth gear was in reach. Jordan had fixed up the transmission so the clutch sang like a dream while the turbo roared like a tornado. With the windows rolled up, sweat beaded up on my forehead.

Eight seconds gone, the last gear conquered, and nothing but nerve. Lights on the side from spectators couldn't distract me. I could taste the finish line.

Then. From the crowd. Something. In my lane.

I slammed on the brakes and struggled to maintain control of the wheel. I had no time and a hundred choices to make. I swerved to the right to miss the object, which put me in front of Ali—he had been behind me. I sensed him barely miss me as he roared past to the finish line. I wondered who was there to greet him, because it sure wasn't LT. Behind me, I saw that I'd painted the road black with my tires, and in front of me, I saw the object I'd avoided: LT's wheelchair. I stopped the car, opened the door, and ran toward the chair. It was empty.

I scanned the crowd. LT sat on the ground, a smile on his face. And with him was

Michael, perfectly positioned to have pushed the chair out into my lane.

"Are you crazy? You trying to kill me?" I screamed as I walk over to LT. I was about to explode from a mix of anger and terror. But LT let me get close before he responded calmly.

"I knew you could handle it. You learned to race from the best," he said, looking smug.

"I thought you were trying to look out for me! Now you lost me another car? Are you insane?"

LT hesitated, eyeing me. "Your friend can keep his ride. Ali just won yours, as soon as you can get it out of impound. But I wouldn't risk your friend's wheels again."

I was still staring at him in disbelief when he spoke up again.

"Now let me ask you a question, DeAndre. You just raced for all you've got left, against someone who's cheated you before. Which one of us just put you in danger? Which one of us is the crazy one?"

# CHAPTER NINETEEN

## TWO MONTHS LATER.

"Summer school is going to suck," Jordan shouted over the beeps, dings, dubstep music, and other noise around us.

"I wouldn't know anything about it," Nikki said just before she kissed my cheek, but all I could do was yawn. Jordan yawned too. "Boy, some Saturday night fun you two are," she said with a laugh.

"I'm sorry. Unlike you, we worked all day," I said and let out a loud sigh. Both Jordan and I had put in eight hard, dirty hours at Hautman Import Automotive. We worked in front for the legitimate business on weekends. Hautman kept the stolen parts in the back. I kept that part from Nikki, but that's about the only thing. Trust on the outs was easy with the right people.

"I had two hours of choir practice and piano lessons." She pretended to pout, which just made her cuter. I touched her skinny arms, finally free of other colors. We didn't talk about Ali, LT, or any of it. I had earned enough to get my car out of impound. I'd left it in front of LT's garage to settle the score from the last race.

"Today you had beautiful music, and tonight all this noise!" I shouted to Nikki.

"It's worth it," she shouted back.

"You ready, Jordan?" I asked. He shifted around behind the wheel. I did the same.

*Tick. Tick. Tick.* "Ready? Set? Go!" Nikki shouted.

*Vroom. Vroom.* Our engines roared as we put the gas pedals to the floor.

The wheel felt right, and most of the sounds were close, but it was the smell that was missing. You just can't replicate the smell of burning tires, exhaust fumes, and adrenaline-fueled sweat in an arcade street-racing video game.

# THE HONDA CIVIC

## MODEL HISTORY

In production since 1978, the Honda Civic is one of the world's most popular cars. For commuters and racing enthusiasts alike, the Honda Civic has held its own in two key areas of the automotive world.

Used for racing ever since its release, the Honda Civic has made a name for itself on the racetrack. A sporty model of the Honda Civic, the Si, is a performance compact/hot hatch version of the Civic.

## THE CIVIC AND MODDING

Honda Civic owners looking for increased speed, better handling, and a sportier appearance often make modifications ("modding") to their cars. Honda sells these "mods," which include equipment for better braking, faster acceleration, and a sleeker look.

Many Civic owners opt to install a cold air intake system to make their engines more powerful. These intake systems are said to increase torque and horsepower, and can help save fuel. Suspension systems are also popular mods. A suspension system can make the car more comfortable and faster by eliminating the severity of bumps on the road or the noise of the highway or racetrack.

## THE CIVIC AND THEFT

Theft rates for the Honda Civic have consistently been some of the highest of any vehicle in the U.S. The Civic ranks among the most stolen cars nearly every year. According to a "Hot Wheels" report from August 2012, the 1998 Honda Civic was the second most-stolen car in America in 2011.

The highest theft rate of any year for the Civic was 2000, when the rate of theft was 5.3269. This means that out of a group of any 100 Civics, over five were stolen that year on average. 2009 had the Civic's lowest rate of theft on record: 0.7830—only ¾ of a Honda Civic was stolen, on average, out of a group of 100.

Car thieves are big fans of the Honda Civic because it is relatively easy to break into and many of its parts are in high demand and can be used in many different makes and models of cars. The most common motive for stealing a car is to get access to the valuable parts and then to profit from reselling those parts.

Some of the Civic's most sought-after parts are the "after market mods" that are made for the car. An after market mod just refers to the modding an owner performed on his or her car after it was purchased. For instance, the intake systems mentioned earlier are frequently stolen off of Civics because of the high demand for them and because of their high monetary value. Performance gear (usually on the outside of the car) is also commonly stolen because it is easy to remove.

## THE CIVIC TODAY

Honda is hoping to turn some heads in the 2013 racing season with the new Civic WTCC race car. Says driver Tiago Monteiro, "Of course we want to fight for the championship. Now we have a lot of information we have learned, but we still have a lot of work to do during winter. Tests this winter will be very important in order to make the Civic WTCC even better because our rivals will still be strong next year. So, we will have to be faster and stronger."

# DEANDRE'S 2001 HONDA CIVIC LX TYPE-R

**ENGINE:** Honda K-series engine, 1.7 liter, 4 cylinder; 115 horsepower (before the turbo kit was added); i-VTEC motor; 5-speed manual transmission; install cold air intake system, new fuel pump, and hoses; enhanced horsepower with turbo kit; install new fuel rails and regulators.

**DRIVETRAIN:** new drive axle; replace the boots; install new clutch kit; replace transmission lines and flywheel.

**SUSPENSION:** install coilover suspension system and new struts (Coilovers are a much better choice for slamming a car than just cutting the springs. Cutting the springs will definitely lower the car and will improve handling for a short amount of time, but after that, your car will probably be in worse condition handling-wise than it was before the mod.); power steering system flush; install rear camber kit and front and rear sway bars; cat back exhaust system and exhaust headers; use lowering kit springs to get this Civic as close to the ground as possible (this is best for handling since it lowers the center of gravity, making it easier to make sharp turns); in the meantime, tightened Macpherson system struts and springs.

**BRAKES:** install new front and rear brake pads; replace brake lines; install four-wheel disc brakes.

**WHEELS/TIRES:** upgrade to high-performance tires; install steelies and some sweet, lightweight rims; invest in an alignment. (It takes a lot of skill to do this, but Jordan and I will be able to do this on our own someday. It's important to keep your wheels aligned when your car's slammed to prevent rubbing the wheel wells.)

**EXTERIOR:** painted body with fresh coat of black; installed lip kit and lip spoilers; the outside of the Civic looks awesome anyway since it's slammed now!

*INTERIOR:* new steering wheel; new shift knob; floor mats; and remove the rearview mirror, of course.

*ELECTRONICS:* upgrade to a sweet new speaker system; install new fuel injectors; install anti-theft system (I can't have anyone around the east side trying to mess with my tricked-out car!)

## Check out the rest of the TURBOCHARGED series: